YOGA FOR EVERYONE

BREATHING AND MEDITATION

BY LAURA VILLANO, RYT
ILLUSTRATED BY CHRISTOS SKALTSAS

BLUE OWL
BOOKS

TIPS FOR CAREGIVERS

Yoga and meditation help us learn about our breath and body, how the two are connected, and how they can help us acknowledge our feelings without letting them overwhelm us. This awareness can help us navigate different situations at school or at home. Meditation gives us tools to be the best versions of ourselves in every situation.

SOCIAL AND EMOTIONAL GOALS

After reading this book, kids will be able to use breathing and meditation to:

1. Become more aware of their emotions and the physical sensations they produce in the body (self-awareness).

2. Use the techniques included in the text to help manage their emotions and de-stress (self-management).

TIPS FOR PRACTICE

Encourage self-awareness and self-management with these prompts:

Before reading: Ask students to check in with themselves. How do they feel, in both mind and body?
Emotional example: What kinds of thoughts are you having?
Physical example: How does your body feel today?

During reading: Encourage students to check in as they move through the book.
Emotional example: How does it feel when you close your eyes and focus on your breathing?
Physical example: How do breathing exercises feel in your body?

After reading: Take time to reflect after practicing the meditation.
Emotional example: How do you feel after practicing breathing and meditation?
Physical example: Are there certain exercises you like or don't like?

TABLE OF CONTENTS

BEFORE YOU BEGIN YOUR PRACTICE, YOU WILL NEED:

· A cushion, mat, or pillow
· Comfy clothes so you can move around easily
· A good attitude and an open mind!

By practicing the exercises in this book, you understand any physical activity has some risk of injury. If you experience pain or discomfort, please listen to your body, discontinue activity, and ask for help.

CHAPTER 1

WHAT IS YOGA?

Namaste (nah-mah-stay)! This is how we greet each other when we practice **yoga**. It is a welcoming greeting. When people say it, they often place their palms together in front of their chest and slightly bow their head.

Yoga is a **sequence** of body movements. It helps our bodies feel calm, relaxed, and ready to sit in **meditation**.

An important part of yoga is breathing. We use it to guide us as we move our bodies. Do you want to practice breathing and meditation?

CHAPTER 2

BREATHING EXERCISES

Our breath keeps us alive. We breathe all day long, even when we are asleep. We do it without thinking!

CONNECT WITH YOUR BREATH

❯ Take a seat on the floor, a cushion, or a chair.

❯ Place your hands in your lap.

❯ Close your eyes or find a still object to **focus** your eyes on.

❯ Breathe in and out.

❯ Do you feel your breath in your nostrils and in your belly? Is your breath shallow or deep?

LION'S BREATH

❯ Sit back on your heels and rest your hands in your lap.

❯ Draw your shoulders down your back.

❯ **Inhale** through your nose.

❯ Look up toward the ceiling.

❯ Open your mouth wide and curl your tongue out toward your chin.

❯ **Exhale** through your mouth and make a "haaaa" sound.

❯ Practice this 5 times!

DID YOU KNOW?

Roaring like a lion is fun, but this exercise can also help you feel awake! It also stretches and relaxes the muscles in your face.

ALTERNATE NOSTRIL BREATHING

❯ Find a comfortable seated position and place your right hand in front of your face.

❯ Inhale and use your right thumb to cover your right nostril.

❯ Exhale and inhale through your left nostril.

❯ Use your right ring finger to cover your left nostril. Release your thumb from your right nostril.

❯ Exhale and inhale through your right nostril to start the **breath cycle** again!

❯ Practice this 5 to 10 times!

TIP: Try this before you take a test! It can help you **concentrate**.

HOW ARE YOU FEELING?

Are you nervous or upset about something? If the answer is yes, stop what you are doing and breathe!

Step back. Find a quiet place to take a moment to focus on your breath.

Find a comfortable seat.
Slowly inhale. Slowly exhale.
Repeat as many times as you need.

CHAPTER 3

MEDITATION

We experience many different **emotions** and **situations** in a given day. Sometimes we are in uncomfortable situations. Sometimes our emotions **overwhelm** us.

Meditation helps us slow down and pay attention to the present moment. It is a great tool to help us respond to situations thoughtfully rather than reacting to them in the heat of the moment. It can help us remember that the discomfort is only **temporary**.

Let's meditate!

BREATH-AWARENESS MEDITATION

❯ Find a comfortable seated position on the floor, on a cushion, or in a chair.

❯ Sit tall and draw your shoulders down your back.

❯ Rest your hands in your lap.

❯ Close your eyes or find a still object to focus your eyes on.

❯ Begin counting your breaths. Inhale = 1. Exhale = 2. Count your inhales and exhales until you count to 10.

❯ Start your counting over. Practice this meditation for 5 to 10 minutes.

As thoughts come up during your meditation,
notice them like you notice clouds in the sky.

You see them, and then they pass by.

Closing a yoga practice with meditation gives you time to **reflect** on the exercise and acknowledge how you feel before moving on with your day.

We live busy lives and are often going from one activity to the next. Meditation helps us pause. Notice how it feels to sit still for a moment without movement. Letting your body and mind be still helps you relax and reset.

What happens when you give yourself time every day for meditation?

GOALS AND TOOLS

GROW WITH GOALS

Try bringing breathing and meditation into your daily life. Here are some ideas to get you started. You can set your own goals, too.

1. Do a body scan before bed every night for a week. How does it change your nighttime routine? How does it change your sleep?

2. Practice a 5-minute meditation at the same time of day for a week. Does meditation change how you move through your day?

BODY SCAN

A body scan is a great way to become familiar with your body. Lie comfortably on the floor or a mat. If it feels good, close your eyes. Focus on your breath.

As you move through the body scan, send your breath to places you feel aches and pains to help them relax. Spend 3 to 5 breath cycles in each area of your body.

- Check in with your feet, toes, and ankles.
- Now bring your attention to your calves, shins, and knees.
- Move your awareness to the upper legs and hips.
- Now think about completely relaxing your legs.
- Let your back and belly feel heavy on the floor.
- Then do the same with your ribs and mid-back.
- Move to your chest and upper back.
- Check in with your shoulders and upper arms.
- Now move your attention to your elbows and forearms.
- Bring your attention to your wrists, hands, and fingers.
- Completely relax both of your arms.
- Work your awareness to your neck.
- Focus on the back of your neck and throat.
- Bring your attention to your face and relax.
- Your head should feel heavy on the floor or mat.
- Rest here for as long as you want. How do you feel?

GLOSSARY

breath cycle
In one breath cycle, air moves in and out of the lungs.

concentrate
To give all of your thought and attention to something.

emotions
Feelings, such as happiness, anger, or sadness.

exhale
To breathe out.

focus
To concentrate on something.

inhale
To breathe in.

meditation
The act of thinking deeply and quietly.

namaste
A common greeting in yoga. It means, "The spirit in me honors and acknowledges the spirit in you."

overwhelm
To have a very strong emotional effect.

reflect
To think carefully or seriously about something.

sequence
A series or collection of things that follow each other in a particular order.

situations
The circumstances that exist at particular times and places.

temporary
Lasting for only a short time.

yoga
A system of exercises and meditation that helps people control their minds and bodies and become physically fit.

TO LEARN MORE

FACT SURFER

Finding more information is as easy as 1, 2, 3.

1. Go to www.factsurfer.com

2. Enter "**breathingandmeditation**" into the search box.

3. Choose your cover to see a list of websites.

INDEX

Blue Owl Books are published by Jump!, 5357 Penn Avenue South, Minneapolis, MN 55419, www.jumplibrary.com

Copyright © 2020 Jump! International copyright reserved in all countries. No part of this book may be reproduced in any form without written permission from the publisher.

Library of Congress Cataloging-in-Publication Data

Names: Villano, Laura, author.
Title: Breathing and meditation / By Laura Villano.
Description: Minneapolis: Jump!, Inc., [2020]
Series: Yoga for everyone
Includes index.
Audience: Ages 7–10
Identifiers: LCCN 2019035846 (print)
LCCN 2019035847 (ebook)
ISBN 9781645272236 (hardcover)
ISBN 9781645272243 (paperback)
ISBN 9781645272250 (ebook)
Subjects: LCSH: Breathing exercises–Juvenile literature.
Meditation–Juvenile literature. | Hatha yoga–Juvenile literature. | Social learning–Juvenile literature.
Classification: LCC RA782 .V55 2020 (print)
LCC RA782 (ebook) | DDC 613/.192–dc23
LC record available at https://lccn.loc.gov/2019035846
LC ebook record available at https://lccn.loc.gov/2019035847

Editor: Jenna Trnka
Designer: Anna Peterson
Illustrator: Christos Skaltsas

Printed in the United States of America at Corporate Graphics in North Mankato, Minnesota.